MY FIRST BOOK OF

MACHINES

with thanks to
Frances Ridley

Caroline Bingham, Bill Gunston, David Kimb

Jeff Painter and Steve Parker

MY FIRST BOOK OF

MACHINES

North American copyright © **ticktock Entertainment Ltd 2008**

First published in North America in 2008 by **ticktock Media Ltd.,**

Unit 2, Orchard Business Centre, North Farm Road, Tunbridge Wells, Kent, TN2 3XF

ISBN 978 1 84696 826 6 pbk

Printed in China

Picture credits

OFC= outside front cover, t=top, b=bottom, c=centre, l-left, r=right
Ainscough Crane Hire: 32–33. Alamy: 78–79, 80b. Alvey & Towers: 28–29c, 46–47. Aviation Picture Library: 86–87, 88–89c, 90–91. Beken of Cowes: 58–59c. British Antarctic Survey: 54–55. Bronto: 68–69. Caterpillar: 40–41. Check-6 images: 80–81. John Clark Photography: 52–53. Corbis: 5t, 5ct, 30–31, 56–57, 59t, 60–61, 84–85, 89b. Sylvia Corday Photo Library: 77t. John Deere: 50–51. JCB: 44–45. Komatsu: OFC, 5b, 34–35, 38–39. Letourneau Inc: 36–37. Mack trucks: 30c. NASA: 92–93. Oshkosh: 5cb, 42–43, 48–49, 66–67. Peterbilt: 28c. RNLI: 64–65, 82–83. Robinson Helicopters: 70–71. Peter Slingsby Systems: 76–77c. The Car Photo Library: 4t, 4b, 6–7, 8–9, 10–11, 12–13, 14–15, 16–17, 18–19, 22–23, 24–25, 26–27. US Coastguard: 72–73, 74–75. Yamaha: 62–63.

Every effort has been made to trace the copyright holders, and we apologize in advance for any unintentional omissions. We would be pleased to insert the appropriate acknowledgments in any subsequent edition of this publication.

CONTENTS

Words that appear in **bold** are explained in the glossary.

FANTASTIC MACHINES

This book is all about things that go! Inside you will find amazing facts about some of the fastest, **BIGGEST** and most exciting machines in the world.

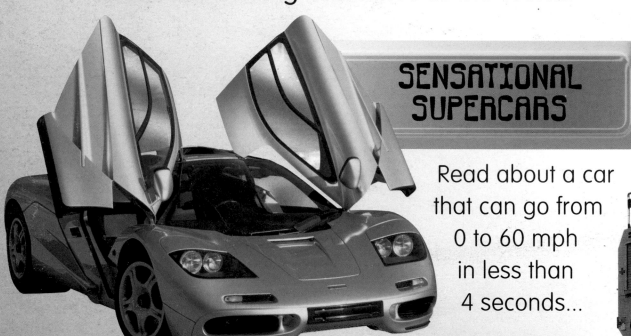

SENSATIONAL SUPERCARS

Read about a car that can go from 0 to 60 mph in less than 4 seconds...

SPEEDY SUPERBIKES

...a motorbike that can drive at over 200 mph...

BRILLIANT BOATS

...a boat that is as long as three soccer pitches....

POWERFUL PLANES

...an airliner that can carry 555 passengers...

EXCITING EMERGENCY VEHICLES

...a giant fire truck that fights fires at airports...

TERRIFIC TRUCKS AND DIGGERS

...and the biggest bulldozer in the world!

FERRARI

Ferrari is famous for making sports cars. Ferrari had been making sports cars for 50 years in 1996. They made a special car to celebrate. The car was called the F50!

A Ferrari F50

TPV 16

The car's **body**, doors, and seats are made from **carbon fiber**.

The **tailpipes** stick out of holes in the back—just like a racing car!

The **engine** is in the middle of the F50. It is nearly as powerful as a **Formula One** engine.

DID YOU KNOW?

The F50 can go from 0 mph to 150 mph in 18 seconds!

BUGATTI

Bugatti was once the biggest car maker in the world. The company was started by Ettore Bugatti. The EB110 was named after him.

The car's **body** is made of **carbon fiber**. There were some bodies left over when the company shut down. They were used to make another supercar.

A Bugatti EB110

The EB110
looks modern.
But it has a wooden
dashboard—just like
an old sports car!

MACHINE FACTFILE

LAUNCHED:
1991

MADE IN:
France

TOP SPEED:
209 mph

ACCELERATION:
0 – 60 mph
in 3.4 seconds

WEIGHT:
1.71 tons

DID YOU KNOW?

Ettore Bugatti
was Italian but
he lived in France.
He built his
factory there.

JAGUAR

Jaguar made the XJ220S in 1994.

It was very fast. The XJ220S cost $578,000.

That was much cheaper than other **supercars**.

A Jaguar XJ220S

The XJ220S has a huge wing at the back. It is very wide for a sports car.

DID YOU KNOW?

When it was made in 1994 the XJ220S was the fastest road car in the world.

The car was based on a Le Mans racing car. Le Mans is a famous race in France.

MACHINE FACTFILE

LAUNCHED:
1994

MADE IN:
UK

TOP SPEED:
217 mph

ACCELERATION:
0 – 60 mph
in 3.3 seconds

WEIGHT:
1.19 tons

The XJ220S has a **body** made of **carbon fiber**. This makes it very light.

McLaren

McLaren are famous for making **Formula One** cars. They wanted to make the best **supercar** in the world. The result was the F1.

DID YOU KNOW?

The F1 was the fastest road car of its time! It was also the most expensive. It cost $1,250,000!

The F1's **engine** is huge.
It takes up all of the back of the car.

Each F1 car took nearly two months to make. McLaren only made 100 F1 cars.

A McLaren F1

The F1 has three seats. It has one in the front and two in the rear. The front seat is in the middle of the car.

MERCEDES-BENZ

Mercedes have been making sports cars for a long time. The Mercedes-Benz SL500 is a **convertible** sports car. The car's roof folds into the trunk when you press a button!

A Mercedes-Benz SL500

DID YOU KNOW?

The car has a sound system and a TV. You turn them on with your voice!

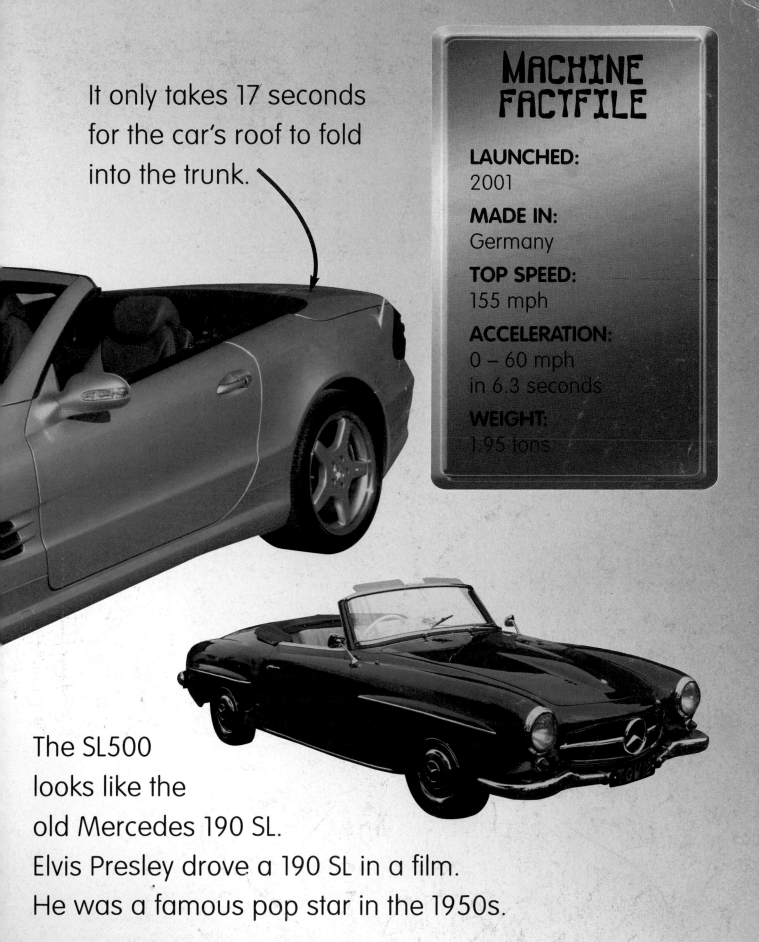

It only takes 17 seconds for the car's roof to fold into the trunk.

MACHINE FACTFILE

LAUNCHED:
2001

MADE IN:
Germany

TOP SPEED:
155 mph

ACCELERATION:
0 – 60 mph
in 6.3 seconds

WEIGHT:
1.95 tons

The SL500 looks like the old Mercedes 190 SL. Elvis Presley drove a 190 SL in a film. He was a famous pop star in the 1950s.

PAGANI ZONDA

The Pagani Zonda has a huge **engine**. Its roof is made of glass. The Zonda was named after a wind. The engine is made by AMG. They make racing car engines.

A Pagani Zonda C12 S

DID YOU KNOW?

You get a free pair of driving shoes when you buy a Zonda.

The Zonda doesn't have a trunk. You put your bags behind the seats.

The inside is made of **aluminum**, **suede**, leather and **carbon fiber**.

MACHINE FACTFILE

LAUNCHED:
2001

MADE IN:
Italy

TOP SPEED:
220 mph

ACCELERATION:
0 – 60 mph
in 3.7 seconds

WEIGHT:
1.37 tons

This car's **tailpipe** looks like a rocket. The car looks like a fighter plane!

TUSCAN

TVR are a company that makes sports cars in England. The first Tuscan was made in 2000. It is has a huge **engine**!

A TVR Tuscan

To open the door you press a little button under the wing mirror.

DID YOU KNOW?

When it was first made the Tuscan cost under $80,000. A good price for a sports car!

The roof and rear window can be taken off! They will fit into the car's large trunk.

GDB 341

The Tuscan's engine fills up all the space under the hood!

THE HAYABUSA

The Hayabusa is made by Suzuki. It is named after a Japanese bird of prey because it is fast and powerful.

The Hayabusa's **engine** is bigger than many car engines!

Suzuki GSX-R100 Hayabusa

Suzuki GSX-1300R Hayabusa

DID YOU KNOW?

A turbo-charged Hayabusa was recorded going faster than 241 mph!

The Hayabusa GSX-R100 has the same top speed as the GSX-1300R. But it has better **acceleration** because it is lighter.

MACHINE FACTFILE

LAUNCHED:
1998

MADE IN:
Japan

GEARS:
6

WEIGHT:
473 lb

TOP SPEED:
186 mph

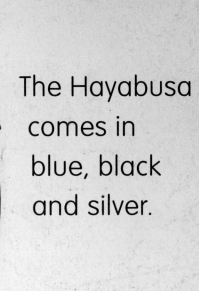

The Hayabusa comes in blue, black and silver.

ARTICULATED TRUCKS

Articulated trucks are the biggest road trucks in the world. The front part of the truck is called the tractor. The back parts are called trailers.

The Peterbilt 379 road truck is an articulated truck. Peterbilt are famous for making trucks.

A Peterbilt 379 road truck

The huge **engine** is at the front of the truck. It is inside a long **hood**.

The hood tips forward. This lets you get to the engine easily.

DID YOU KNOW?

Truck drivers may drive for many days. Some trucks have a bed in the tractor.

ROAD TRAINS

A road train is a truck that pulls three or more trailers. A road train carries huge loads from city to city.

A company called Mack makes road trains. The biggest Mack truck is called the Titan.

Mack trucks have a bulldog badge on the front.

Road trains have big **radiators**. They cool the engine down.

A Mack road train

DID YOU KNOW?

The most powerful Mack truck has a gold bulldog badge. The other Mack trucks have a silver badge.

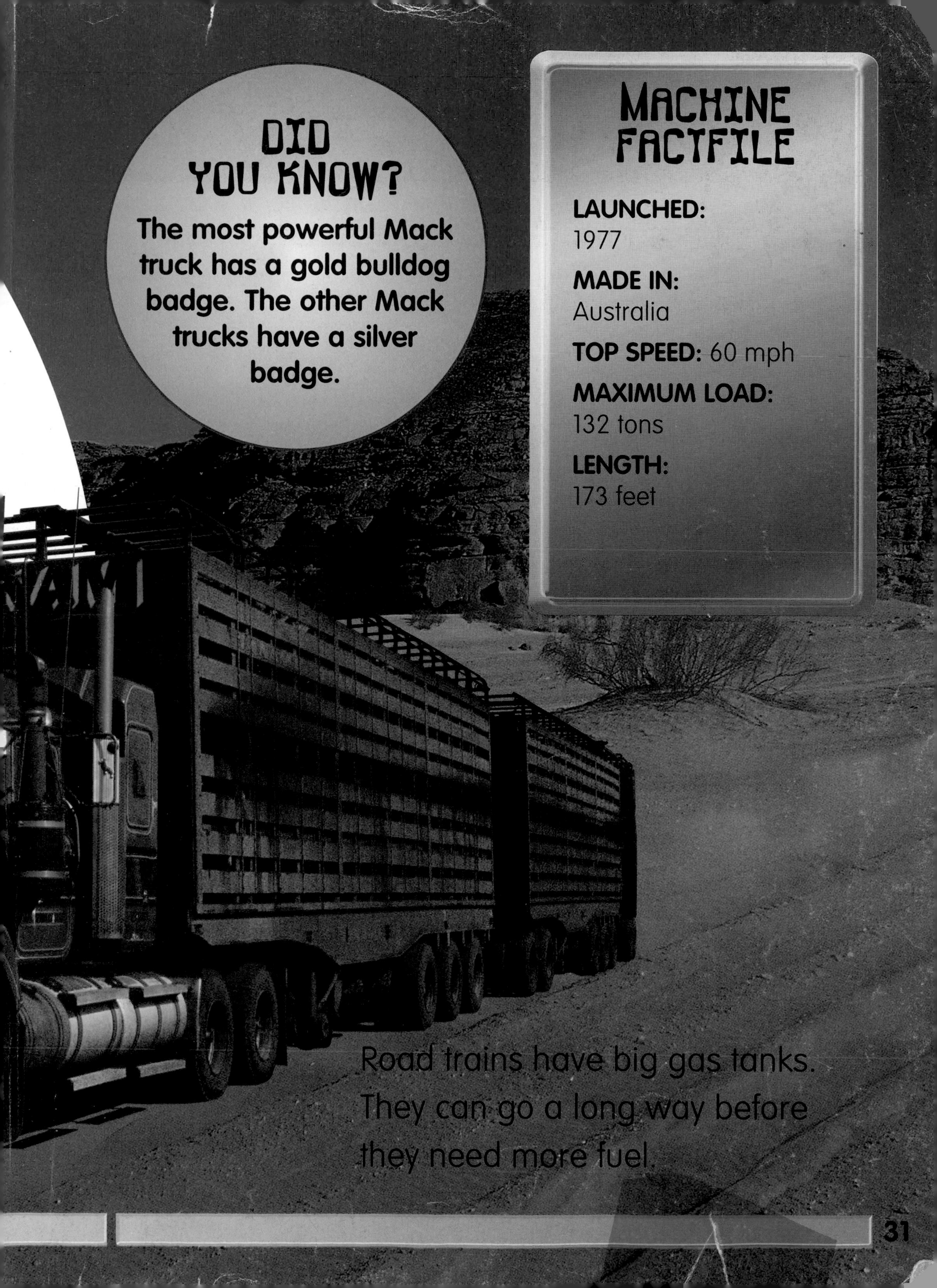

MACHINE FACTFILE

LAUNCHED:
1977

MADE IN:
Australia

TOP SPEED: 60 mph

MAXIMUM LOAD:
132 tons

LENGTH:
173 feet

Road trains have big gas tanks. They can go a long way before they need more fuel.

CRANES

Cranes are used to lift heavy loads. Some cranes are fixed in the same place. Other cranes are on wheels. You can drive them from place to place.

The Liebherr LTM 1500 puts down four legs when it lifts things.

DID YOU KNOW?

The biggest cranes in the world can lift 881 tons. That's the weight of six blue whales!

The LTM is on wheels.
It can lift the weight of 500 cars!

MACHINE FACTFILE

LAUNCHED:
2002

MADE IN:
Germany

TOP SPEED: 50 mph

MAXIMUM LOAD:
551 tons

LIFTING HEIGHT:
574 feet

Cranes have a hook
for lifting things.

A Liebherr LTM 1500 crane

A crane's arm
is called a jib.

DUMP TRUCKS

Dump trucks are used to carry heavy loads **on site**. They do not go on roads.

This huge dump truck is made by Komatsu. It is called the Haulpak 930E. The wheels are nearly nine feet tall!

A Haulpak 930E dump truck

DID YOU KNOW?

The driver has to climb up these steps to get to the cab!

The truck works in **quarries** and **mines**. It carries huge loads of rock, earth, and coal.

MACHINE FACTFILE

LAUNCHED:
1996

MADE IN:
Japan

TOP SPEED: 40 mph

MAXIMUM LOAD:
358 tons

WEIGHT OF EACH TIRE:
5.1 tons

OE

The bucket is made of **steel**. Six big cars could fit in the bucket!

WHEEL LOADERS

A wheel loader digs up earth and rocks.

Then it dumps them into the back of a truck.

The wheel loader uses a bucket to dig.

DID YOU KNOW?

The L-2350 wheel loader has huge tires. They are 13 feet tall. That's taller than three children put together!

EXCAVATORS

Excavators are digging machines.

A company called Caterpillar makes lots of excavators. Some are small and some are large. The Cat 385L is huge!

The excavator's arm has three parts. At the end is the bucket. The bucket has teeth that dig into the ground.

The LeTourneau L-2350 is the biggest wheel loader in the world. A car could fit into its bucket.

MACHINE FACTFILE

LAUNCHED:
2001

MADE IN:
USA

TOP SPEED: 10.5 mph

MAXIMUM LOAD:
79 tons

BUCKET WIDTH:
22 feet 4 inches

The driver sits in the cab. He uses a joystick. The joystick makes the bucket dig and dump.

A LeTourneau L-2350 wheel loader

BULLDOZERS

Bulldozers break up earth and push it around. The Komatsu D575A Super Dozer is huge. It is twice as big as any other bulldozer.

The Super Dozer has a Super Ripper! The Super Ripper can break up 2,200 tons of earth an hour. Its teeth are more than three feet long.

A Komatsu D575A Super Dozer

The Super Dozer's blade is 24 feet wide.

The Super Dozer has speci tracks. They help it to go o muddy or bumpy groun

DID YOU KNOW?

The bright yellow color is called 'Highway yellow'. It stands out well from the other traffic.

MACHINE FACTFILE

LAUNCHED:
1991

MADE IN:
USA

TOP SPEED: 4.4 mph

HEIGHT OF CAB:
12 feet

WEIGHT:
92 tons

The cab is where the driver sits. The cab can turn all the way round.

A CAT 385L Excavator

The tracks help the Cat 385L to drive over bumpy and muddy ground.

MIXER TRUCKS

A mixer truck makes concrete. It mixes the concrete as it travels to the construction site. When it arrives, the concrete is ready to use!

DID YOU KNOW?
Concrete is made from gravel, sand, cement and water.

This is an Oshkosh mixer. It sends the concrete down this **chute**.

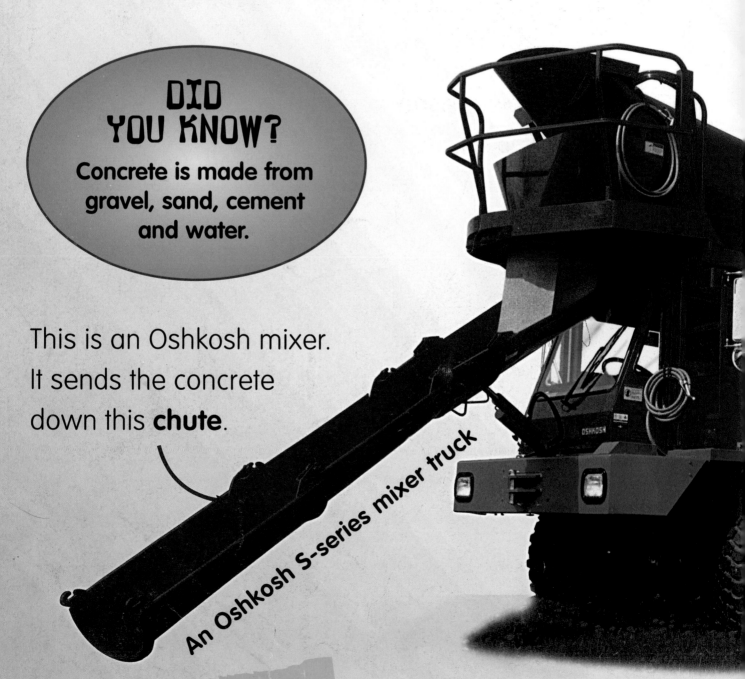

An Oshkosh S-series mixer truck

MACHINE FACTFILE

LAUNCHED:
1999

MADE IN:
USA

TOP SPEED: 50 mph

CHUTE LENGTH:
21 feet

LENGTH:
39 feet

This drum is where the concrete is mixed.

The drum turns round slowly as the mixer truck travels along. The drum is washed with water when it is empty.

BACKHOE LOADERS

A backhoe loader digs a hole with its bucket.

Then it picks up the earth with its **shovel**.

It moves the earth away.

DID YOU KNOW?

The middle of the backhoe loader is just like a tractor.

This backhoe loader is made by JCB. JCB are famous for making trucks and diggers.

This is the shovel.

These are the Dancing Diggers! They do stunts and shows.

MACHINE FACTFILE

LAUNCHED:
1962

MADE IN:
UK

TOP SPEED: 67 mph

SHOVEL WIDTH:
7.5 feet

LENGTH:
18 feet

This is the bucket. It can work at the back or the side of the loader.

A JCB backhoe loader

BREAKDOWN TRUCKS

A breakdown truck rescues broken-down trucks. The breakdown truck fixes a winch on to the broken-down truck. Then it pulls the truck to the garage to be mended.

This breakdown truck was used to rescue army tanks. It has a huge **engine** and is very strong.

MACHINE FACTFILE

LAUNCHED:
1985

MADE IN:
Germany

TOP SPEED: 60 mph

WEIGHT:
22 tons

LENGTH:
39 feet

Sometimes breakdown trucks rescue trucks at night.
They need very bright lights, like these.

SUTTON BRIDGE, LINCS.

800 7312905

24 HOUR SERVICE

CAR & COMMERCIAL
TEARS RECOVERY
RECOVERY SPECIALISTS

A Mercedes recovery truck

SNOW MOVERS

Snow movers get snow off the roads. Oshkosh makes lots of snow movers. They move the snow in different ways.

This snow mover can push 5,500 tons of snow an hour.

This snow mover has two **engines**. One engine drives the snow mover along. The other engine blows the snow out of the road.

DID YOU KNOW?

Some snow movers sweep the snow. Some blow the snow and some push it.

MACHINE FACTFILE

LAUNCHED:
1991

MADE IN:
USA

TOP SPEED: 45 mph

WEIGHT:
22 tons

LENGTH:
27 feet

The **tailpipe** pipes go straight up into the air.

An Oshkosh snow mover

COMBINE HARVESTERS

A combine harvester works in a wheat field. It harvests the ripe wheat.

It cuts the wheat down. Then it strips the grain from the stalks. The stalks are left behind the combine harvester. They are picked up later.

This combine harvester is made by John Deere. The company's badge shows a deer.

DID YOU KNOW?

It used to take ten men a whole day to harvest a small field. The combine harvester does it in one hour!

MACHINE FACTFILE

LAUNCHED:
1999

MADE IN:
USA

TOP SPEED: 20 mph

MAXIMUM LOAD:
2,792 gallons of grain

LENGTH:
32 feet

The grain is stored in this large tank.

These blades cut the wheat down.

DRAG BOATS

Drag boats are the fastest racing boats. They are more like rockets than boats. The Californian Quake drag boat can go at 230 mph!

DID YOU KNOW?
The Californian Quake can travel ¼ mile in under 5 seconds!

The top of the boat breaks off if there is a crash. This helps the driver to escape.

The driver's helmet is linked to a bottle of air. The driver can breathe underwater if he has a crash.

The Californian Quake

Drag boats only hold one person.

RESEARCH SHIPS

Research ships explore new places. They find out all about them.

31 scientists work on the James Clark Ross research ship. The boat also carries 15 **crew**, 12 **officers** and a doctor.

The James Clark Ross

The James Clark Ross is a research ship in **Antarctica.** It finds out about the sea and the weather. It looks for strange creatures under the sea!

DID
YOU KNOW?
The James
Clark Ross can
smash through
thick ice!

MACHINE FACTFILE

LAUNCHED:
1990

MADE IN:
UK

WIDTH:
61 feet

LENGTH:
324 feet

TOP SPEED:
18 mph

The **hull** is made of strong **steel**. The ship is very heavy. It weighs 6,318 tons—that's more than 30 jumbo jets put together!

FIREBOATS

Fireboats fight fires on ships and in buildings by the sea and rivers. Sometimes ships carry **cargo**, like oil, which can catch alight.

Six powerful pumps suck in water from around the boat. The water is fired out of water-guns.

A Los Angeles fireboat

All parts of the fireboat are **flameproof**.

2 LOS ANGELES CITY FIRE D

Fireboats don't spray water on electrical fires. They spray special foam instead.

MACHINE FACTFILE

LAUNCHED:
1925

MADE IN:
USA

WEIGHT:
167 tons

LENGTH:
98 feet

TOP SPEED:
20 mph

DID YOU KNOW?

The boat's water-guns shoot jets of water as high as 492 feet.

AIRCRAFT CARRIERS

Aircraft carriers are warships. The Nimitz-class aircraft carrier is huge. It carries 85 planes and 6 helicopters. It also carries 6,000 **crew** members!

Planes and helicopters need fuel. The fuel is kept in tanks. The tanks are the size of swimming pools!

DID YOU KNOW?

The crew of the Nimitz-class aircraft carrier eat 20,000 meals a day!

A Nimitz-class aircraft carrier

The crew use the latest computers and special machines for tracking other ships and planes.

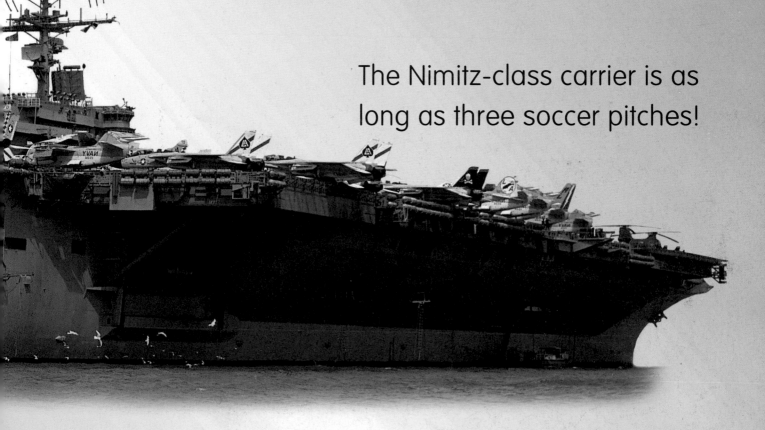

MACHINE FACTFILE

LAUNCHED:
1972

MADE IN:
USA

WEIGHT:
Over 110,000 tons

LENGTH:
1,092 feet

TOP SPEED:
35 mph

The Nimitz-class carrier is as long as three soccer pitches!

OIL SUPERTANKERS

Oil supertankers are the biggest ships in the world. They carry millions of barrels of oil across the sea. The oil can be used to make gas, paint, and plastic.

This is the Jahre Viking supertanker. It has 40 **crew** members. They live in the stern.

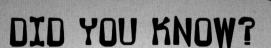

DID YOU KNOW?

Oil supertankers are very slow. The Jahre Viking's top speed is 11.5 mph.

The oil comes from an oil rig. It is pumped on to the tanker through pipes.

MACHINE FACTFILE

LAUNCHED:
1979

MADE IN:
Japan

WEIGHT:
622,544 tons unloaded

LENGTH:
1,502 feet

WIDTH:
226 feet

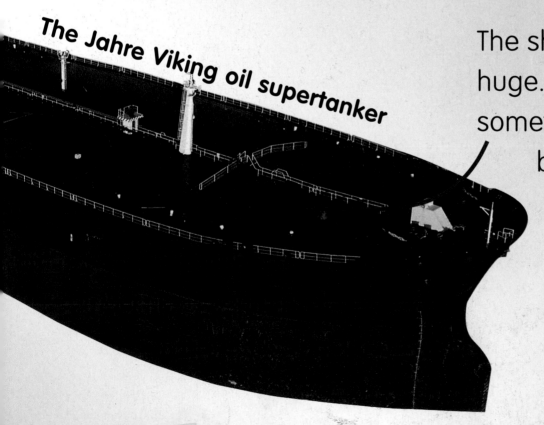

The Jahre Viking oil supertanker

The ship's deck is huge. The crew sometimes use bikes to get around.

JETSKIS

You can ride a jetski over the waves at top speed. You can do stunts on them, too. The jetski stops if you fall off. This lets you get back on again!

The engine sucks water in. Then it blasts the water out in a fast jet. This jet pushes the jetski along.

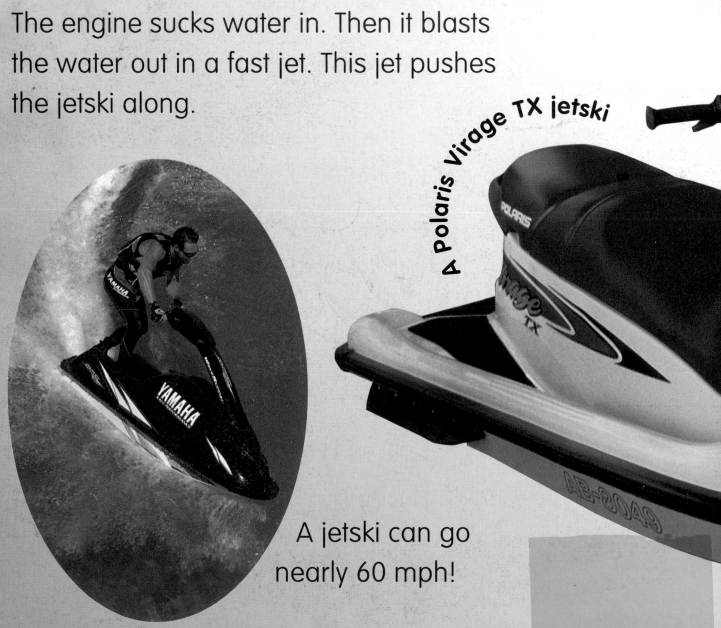

A Polaris Virage TX jetski

A jetski can go nearly 60 mph!

POLARIS

You steer a jetski with handlebars—just like a bike.

LIFEBOATS

Lifeboats rescue people from the sea. Lifeboats have to be strong and their **crews** have to be brave.

The crew use radios and special tracking equipment to find ships that are in trouble.

The boat's **hull** is made of plastic and **carbon fiber**. It is light and does not rust.

MACHINE FACTFILE

LAUNCHED:
1994

MADE IN:
UK

WEIGHT:
30 tons

LENGTH:
45 feet

SPEED:
29 mph

Rescued people sit here. There are heaters to warm them up. There are dry clothes, hot drinks, and snacks.

THE STRIKER

The Striker fights airport fires. It is the biggest fire truck in the world.

The Striker makes a hole in a plane that is on fire. It puts a camera through the hole to see where the fire is. Then it shoots foam through the hole to put the fire out.

The Striker has huge wheels. They help it drive over muddy ground.

The Striker 4500 fire truck

THE BRONTO SKYLIFT

The Bronto Skylift is a fire truck. It has a platform on a very long arm. This helps to fight fires in very tall buildings. It helps firefighters to rescue people trapped inside.

The Bronto Skylift has a thick **steel** hose for spraying water. The hose unfolds with the arm.

A Bronto Skylift fire truck

DID YOU KNOW?

You can use the platform like a crane. It can lift someone out of a building on a stretcher.

MACHINE FACTFILE

LAUNCHED:
2000

MADE IN:
Finland

TOP SPEED:
40 mph

CREW:
5

AMAZING FACT:
It sprays 1,003 gallons of water per minute.

The Bronto Skylift can reach higher than any other fire truck.
This model can reach 236 feet in the air.

R44 HELICOPTER

The R44 helicopter helps the police to do their job. It has a search light, a siren, and a **loud hailer**.

The R44 helicopter

DID YOU KNOW?

The R44 has a special camera. It can film things on the ground when the R44 is flying.

Three people can sit in the R44. The big glass windows let everyone see out.

Helicopter **engines** make a lot of noise. The R44 is padded with special foam. This stops it being too noisy inside.

MACHINE FACTFILE

LAUNCHED:
1993

MADE IN:
USA

NORMAL SPEED:
130 mph

CREW:
2

AMAZING FACT:
The R44 flies 14,000 feet above the ground.

The R44 can go 400 miles on a full tank of fuel. That's very good for a helicopter!

AIRTANKERS

Airtankers fight forest fires.

They drop **fire retardant** on to the fire.

A P-3 Orion firefighting airtanker

The retardant is dropped in a straight line.
The fire won't spread over the line.

The P3's tank is under its body. The pilot uses a computer to open the tank's doors.

DID YOU KNOW?

P-3 Orion airtankers used to be spy planes.

The P-3 Orion is named after a group of stars. The stars show a hunter called Orion.

AIR-SEA RESCUE HELICOPTERS

An air-sea rescue helicopter saves people who get into trouble at sea. It pulls them up on a line. Then it takes them to hospital.

There is a small **blade** on the helicopter's tail. It helps the helicopter to stay in one place in the air.

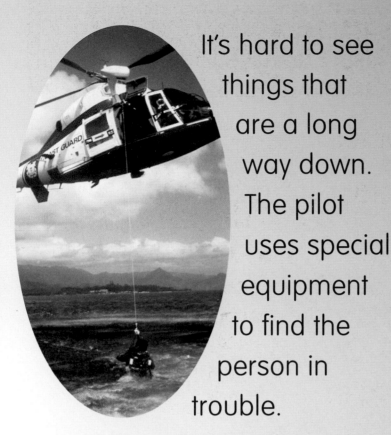

It's hard to see things that are a long way down. The pilot uses special equipment to find the person in trouble.

The HH-60J Jayhawk

MACHINE FACTFILE

LAUNCHED:
1986

MADE IN:
USA

TOP SPEED:
300 mph

CREW:
4

AMAZING FACT:
The Jayhawk can rescue 6 people at once.

The helicopter blades are 19 feet long. They are folded away when the helicopter isn't flying.

RESCUE SUBMERSIBLES

The LR7 is a rescue **submersible**.
It rescues people trapped in **submarines**.

The LR7 goes underwater and finds the submarine. It fixes on to the submarine. The trapped people can move into the LR7 through a special escape door.

DID YOU KNOW?

It's hard to see things underwater. The LR7 uses special equipment to find submarines.

The LR7 can rescue 18 people. They sit in the rescue **chamber** at the back.

LR7 RESCUE SUBMERSIBLE

This is the LR5 submersible. It is being lowered into the water.

MACHINE FACTFILE

LAUNCHED:
2004

MADE IN:
UK

TOP SPEED:
3.5 mph

CREW:
3

AMAZING FACT:
The LR7 is just 31 feet long.

The LR7 rescue submersible

This is where the LR7 fixes on to the submarine.

HAGGLUNDS BV206

The Hagglunds BV206 does lots of different things. It fights fires. It rescues people. It explores deserts and jungles.

The Hagglunds BV206

DID YOU KNOW?

The Hagglunds can float, too! Its top speed in water is 1.86 mph.

The Hagglunds has special tracks. They can go over snow, ice, mud, grass, or sand.

This vehicle rescues people trapped in snow. It pushes the heavy snow out of the way.

LAUNCHED:
1994

MADE IN:
Sweden

TOP SPEED ON LAND:
32 mph

CREW:
2

AMAZING FACT:
It can rescue and carry 10 people at once.

The back can be used as an ambulance. It can also be used to carry soldiers.

HEAVY RESCUE 56 TRUCK

This huge truck is owned by the Los Angeles Fire Department in America. It goes to accidents to do cutting or heavy lifting.

This arm can swing to the side to lift cars out of rivers or ditches.

A Heavy Rescue 56

The winch has 295 feet of thick, **steel** cable.

The lifting equipment can be worked by remote control if it is too dangerous for the **crew** to get close to an accident.

MACHINE FACTFILE

LAUNCHED:
1995

MADE IN:
USA

TOP SPEED:
100 mph

CREW:
5

AMAZING FACT:

This machine can help lift up pieces of buildings that have fallen down.

DID YOU KNOW?

The winch is so strong it can lift something that weighs the same as 15 cars!

ATLANTIC 75 LIFEBOAT

The Atlantic 75 helps rescue people out at sea. It has a hard, plastic **hull** and an inflatable section filled with air on top.

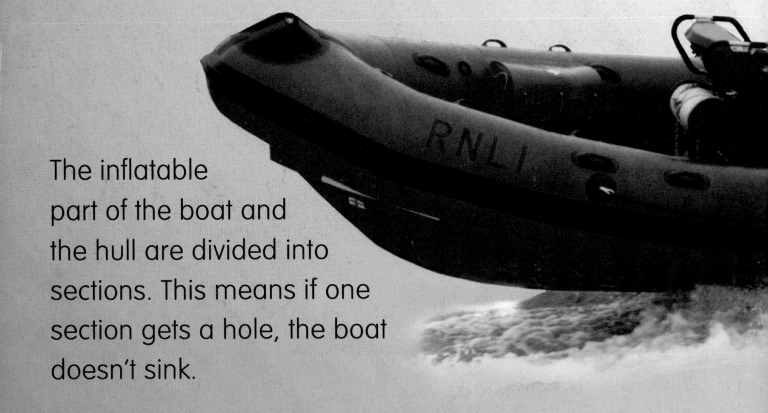

The inflatable part of the boat and the hull are divided into sections. This means if one section gets a hole, the boat doesn't sink.

If the boat turns over, the **crew** pull a cord. This blows up a big airbag which turns the boat the right way up!

MACHINE FACTFILE

LAUNCHED:
1992

MADE IN:
UK

TOP SPEED:
36.82 mph

CREW:
3

AMAZING FACT:
This boat can go 50 miles out to sea to a rescue.

The Atlantic 75 can keep traveling at its top speed for three hours before it needs more fuel.

AIRBUS A380

The Airbus A380 is the largest **airliner** in the world. It carries 555 passengers.

The Airbus A380 has three decks. One deck is for the cargo. The other two decks are for the passengers.

DID YOU KNOW?

The Airbus A380-800F carries cargo, not people. It can carry 165 tons of cargo!

An Airbus A380

MACHINE FACTFILE

LAUNCHED:
2006

MADE IN:
Europe

WING SPAN:
261 feet

LENGTH:
239 feet

TOP SPEED:
647 mph

Passengers can walk around on the Airbus. There are shops and places to eat. There are places for children to play, too!

The Airbus has two engines

THE BLACKBIRD

The SR-71 Blackbird is a spy plane. It has powerful **engines** and is very fast.

The Blackbird carries cameras and **sensors**. The cameras are used to spy on the enemy. The sensors are used to spot enemy planes.

DID YOU KNOW?

The Blackbird flew from New York to London in less than two hours!

The SR-71 Blackbird

The Blackbird was made in top secret.

MACHINE FACTFILE

LAUNCHED:
1962

MADE IN:
USA

WINGSPAN:
52 feet

LENGTH:
101 feet

TOP SPEED:
2,250 mph

The plane is made from a special metal. It keeps the plane cool when it goes very fast.

JUMBO JET

The Boeing 747 is a big, fast **airliner**.

It is known as the jumbo jet.

DID YOU KNOW?

A jumbo jet carries 57,061 gallons of fuel. That would fill up 4,000 cars!

It can carry 412 passengers and 22 **crew**. It can also carry more than 110 tons of **cargo**.

The jumbo jet has four **engines** and 18 wheels.

A Boeing 747

MACHINE FACTFILE

LAUNCHED:
1966

MADE IN:
USA

WINGSPAN:
209 feet

LENGTH:
230 feet

TOP SPEED:
570 mph

The cargo can be loaded through the plane's nose!

THE TYPHOON

The Typhoon is a war plane. It carries a gun, missiles, and bombs. It goes faster than the speed of sound!

A Eurofighter Typhoon

DID YOU KNOW?

It took 20 years to plan and make the Typhoon.

Most of the Typhoon's body is made of **carbon fiber**. It is much lighter than metal. The carbon fiber keeps the plane cool when it goes very fast.

Typhoons come with one or two seats.

MACHINE FACTFILE

LAUNCHED:
2002

MADE IN:
Europe

WINGSPAN:
35 feet

LENGTH:
49 feet

TOP SPEED:
1,323 mph

These two **engines** make the Typhoon very fast. It can take off in five seconds!

THE SPACE SHUTTLE

The shuttle is a space plane. It can be used again and again. The first spacecraft were only used once.

Ten people can travel in the space shuttle.

The Space Shuttle

The space shuttle uses three tanks of fuel. One huge tank launches the shuttle. Then the shuttle uses fuel from two rocket **boosters**. The rocket boosters fall off when they are empty.

MACHINE FACTFILE

LAUNCHED:
1981

MADE IN:
USA

WINGSPAN:
75 feet

LENGTH:
183 feet

TOP SPEED:
17,440 mph

GLOSSARY

acceleration   A change in speed—getting faster!

airliner   A large passenger plane.

aluminum   A very light metal.

Antarctica   An area of the world that is covered in ice and snow.

blades   The parts of a helicopter that spin round.

body   The outside part of a vehicle.

boosters   Fuel tanks that are fixed on to the side of a spacecraft.

brake disk   A part of a vehicle that helps to slow it down.

carbon fiber   A material that is used when a vehicle needs to be made of something strong but light.

cargo   Things carried from one place to another by a truck, plane, or boat.

chamber   Another word for a room.

chute   A slide to take things from one place to another.

convertible   A car that you can drive with the roof up or down.

crew   The people who drive and work in a vehicle.

dashboard   The part of a vehicle that has displays which show how fast it is going and how much gas it has left.

engine   The part of a vehicle that burns fuel and gives it the power to move along.

fire retardant   Something dropped onto fires to stop them spreading, such as foam or water.